EllRay Jakes
is NOT a chicken!

EllRay Jakes
is NOT a chicken!

BY **Sally Warner**

ILLUSTRATED BY
Jamie Harper

VIKING
An Imprint of Penguin Group (USA) Inc.

VIKING
Published by Penguin Group
Penguin Young Readers Group, 345 Hudson Street, New York, New York 10014, U.S.A.
Penguin Group (Canada), 90 Eglinton Avenue East, Suite 700, Toronto, Ontario, Canada M4P 2Y3
(a division of Pearson Penguin Canada Inc.)
Penguin Books Ltd, 80 Strand, London WC2R 0RL, England
Penguin Ireland, 25 St Stephen's Green, Dublin 2, Ireland (a division of Penguin Books Ltd)
Penguin Group (Australia), 250 Camberwell Road, Camberwell, Victoria 3124, Australia
(a division of Pearson Australia Group Pty Ltd)
Penguin Books India Pvt Ltd, 11 Community Centre, Panchsheel Park, New Delhi – 110 017, India
Penguin Group (NZ), 67 Apollo Drive, Rosedale, North Shore 0632,
New Zealand (a division of Pearson New Zealand Ltd.)
Penguin Books (South Africa) (Pty) Ltd, 24 Sturdee Avenue, Rosebank, Johannesburg 2196, South Africa

Penguin Books Ltd, Registered Offices: 80 Strand, London WC2R 0RL, England

First published in 2011 by Viking, a division of Penguin Young Readers Group

1 3 5 7 9 10 8 6 4 2

Text copyright © Sally Warner, 2011
Interior illustrations copyright © Jamie Harper, 2011
Cover illustration copyright © Brian Biggs, 2011
All rights reserved

LIBRARY OF CONGRESS CATALOGING-IN-PUBLICATION DATA
Warner, Sally.
EllRay Jakes is not a chicken / by Sally Warner ; illustrated by Jamie Harper.
p. cm.
Summary: Eight-year-old EllRay's father has promised a family trip to Disneyland if EllRay can stay out of
trouble for a week, but not defending himself against Jared, the class bully, proves to be a real challenge.
ISBN 978-0-670-06243-0 (hardcover)
[1. Behavior—Fiction. 2. Bullies—Fiction. 3. Schools—Fiction. 4. Family life—California—Fiction.
5. California—Fiction.] I. Harper, Jamie, ill. II. Title.
PZ7.W24644Em 2011
[Fic]—dc22
2010025106

Manufactured in China
Set in ITC Century
Book design by Nancy Brennan

For my long-time editor, Tracy Gates,

with affection and gratitude—S.W.

For Peter and Charles—J.H.

CONTENTS

☒ ☒ ☒

EllRay Jakes
is <u>NOT</u> a chicken!

1

TWO FOR FLINCHING

"Two for flinching," Jared Matthews says at lunch one **MONDAY** in January. **BOP!** He punches me really hard on my right arm muscle—which is not very big, it's true.

It looks like a ping-pong ball, only brown.

"I didn't flinch," I argue, rubbing my arm to make the sting go away.

My name is EllRay Jakes, and I am eight years old. I am the smallest kid in Ms. Sanchez's third grade class, even counting the girls, and Jared is the biggest.

It's like I am made out of sticks, and Jared is made out of logs.

My dad says I'm going to get bigger someday, but when?

"Here's one to grow on, EllRay," Jared's kiss-up

friend Stanley Washington says, his glasses gleaming like mean lizard eyes.

And—*BOP!*

"EllRay *wishes* he would grow," Jared says—because I'm so short. Great joke, Jared.

And then Jared laughs like a cartoon donkey: **"HAW, HAW, HAW!"**

It's just another relaxing lunch on an ordinary day at Oak Glen Primary School, in Oak Glen, California.

✕ ✕ ✕

There is a third grade boys' war going on at our school, but the three kids in the war—Jared Matthews, Stanley Washington, and me, EllRay Jakes—all act like nothing is wrong.

Our teacher, Ms. Sanchez, doesn't have a clue.

Ms. Sanchez is smart about what goes on *inside* her classroom, but she doesn't know what goes on outside—before school and during nutrition break, lunch, and afternoon recess.

And outside is when school really happens for kids.

"Good one, Stanley," Jared says after Stanley insults me, and Jared high-fives him.

"Bad one, Stanley," I echo, trying to make fun of them.

Stanley Washington is like Jared's shadow. He wears glasses, like I said, and he has straight brown hair that flops over his forehead as if it has given up trying.

Jared is chunky and strong, and he has frowning eyes, and his brown hair sticks up all over the place like a cat just licked it.

His hair does whatever it wants, just like Jared.

A couple of girls hop by, holding hands. Jared and Stanley step back, looking all innocent—because girls *tell*. Especially these girls, Cynthia Harbison and *her* kiss-up friend Heather Patton.

"Icky boys," Cynthia calls out over her shoulder.

Cynthia is the cleanest person I have ever met. She is strangely clean.

For instance, Cynthia's fingernails never have any dirt under them. Also, her clothes never get any food, poster paint, or grass stains on them, no matter what. I don't think she has very much fun,

and what's the point in being that clean if it means you never get to have any fun?

Cynthia has short, straight hair that she holds back with a plastic hoop, and Heather pulls *her* long hair back so tight in a ponytail that her eyes always look scared. But maybe Heather really *is* scared— from hanging around mean, bossy Cynthia all the time!

Cynthia is like Jared, only without the hitting.

"Hey, EllRay, why don't you go sit on the grass with the rest of the girls?" Jared asks me when Cynthia and Heather have hopped away to the other side of the playground.

"Yeah, crybaby," Stanley says. "Go sit with the girls."

"I'm not even crying, *Stanley-ella*," I say, pretending *he* is the girl.

It's the best put-down I can come up with on such short notice.

"That's not even my name, so duh," Stanley says.

"*DUH*," I say back at him.

I want to turn around and walk away. But if I do, Jared will probably grab me from the back, tight, and start grinding his knuckles into my ribs.

This is one of his favorite things to do, because from far away, you can't tell anything bad is going on.

Jared's supreme goal is to make me cry someday— in front of the entire class.

So I have to wait for Jared and Stanley to be the ones to walk away first.

I would rather be playing kickball with Corey Robinson and Kevin McKinley, who are my friends, but it's not exactly like I have a choice right now.

"*Duh*," I say again. I don't know why.

Finally, finally, *finally* the recess bell rings, and Jared gives Stanley a friendly pretend-shove, and Stanley gives Jared a shove too, only not as hard, because Jared is the boss. And they walk away without even looking at me.

Like I'm nothing!

"Come on, EllRay," Emma McGraw says as she skips by with red-haired Annie Pat Masterson. "We have Spanish this afternoon, and Ms. Sanchez is going to talk about food. Taquitos, burritos, and enchiladas and stuff. Yum!"

Emma is the second-littlest kid in our class, but she loves to eat. I think it's her main hobby.

"Hurry up," Annie Pat calls out, and she and Emma skip away.

And so I hurry up. But I don't skip, because boys just *don't*. Not at Oak Glen Primary School, anyway.

And probably not anywhere.

Not when they have arm muscles the size of ping-pong balls.

I CAN'T EXPLAIN

Okay. I can't explain why Jared and Stanley started their war against me, but who cares why the war started? Details like that don't really matter, not when someone is secretly grinding his fist into your ribs.

I know *when* it began, though. It began two weeks ago, right after Christmas vacation.

Why don't I tell somebody what is happening?

Because it wouldn't do any good, and here's why:

1. If the other boys in our class knew about this three-person war, they would take sides, and then it would just turn into a bigger war. But it wouldn't be over for me.

2. If the girls in our class knew, they would whisper and stare, and I hate that.

3. If my mom knew what was happening, she would probably call Jared's mother and complain. And of course that would only make things worse for me in the long run.

4. If my dad knew about our war, he would FREAK OUT. First, he would call Ms. Sanchez or the principal. Then they would make a big announcement to the whole class about fighting, and then the grown-ups would study the problem to death, because studying things is what my dad likes best in the whole wide world.

But there's nothing to study about why Jared hates me. I think he's just bored, and he is taking it out on me.

Or maybe beating me up was Jared's New Year's resolution.

Our war started for no reason, and it will probably end for no reason.

I just have to live through it, that's all.

But the point is, this is a terrible Monday. And I know it sounds dumb, but I am a kid who usually likes Mondays—because Monday gives you a brand-new start.

Monday is like a spelling test that your teacher has just passed out, and you haven't had time yet to make any mistakes. It's like a blank piece of art paper that you haven't messed up. Monday is like the second after your teacher asks you a mental math question in front of the whole class—but you haven't given the wrong answer. *Yet.*

Any good thing can happen on a Monday!

Not this Monday, though.

✻ **3** ✻

"BEHAVIOR:
NEEDS IMPROVEMENT"

"You don't have to keep saying it, Dad, because I already promised," I tell my father that night after dinner, which was pork chops and mashed potatoes, and some kind of vegetable that I spread around on my plate so it at least looked half-eaten.

I am trying to keep my voice calm, steady, and well-behaved.

Dr. Warren Jakes—also known as Dad—is giving me a "talking-to," which is the same talking-to I've been getting from him ever since my progress report came out last week.

"Behavior: Needs improvement," Ms. Sanchez wrote.

Teachers never think about what happens *after* they send home a report card or a note, because writing that comment in my progress report was like telling my dad that his hair was on fire.

My father is a big, strong guy who wears glasses. He is also very smart. He is a college professor who teaches geology in San Diego.

Geology is rocks, basically.

Teaching about rocks must be the most boring job in the whole world. *Do not tell anyone I said this!* But I wish he were a fireman—or a professional extreme snowboarder.

That would be a whole lot cooler, if you ask me.

But even though his job is usually pretty boring, like I just said, my dad and I sometimes get to go on really fun camping trips to Utah, Arizona, and Nevada, where we collect specimens and eat hot dogs and s'mores.

We've seen rattlesnakes and tarantulas and wild pigs called javelinas!

I love to do alone stuff with my dad.

The only bad thing about my dad is that I think he wants me to be a shorter version of him: smart, serious, and sensible.

I think he might even want me to become a geologist some day.

Don't get your hopes up, Dad!

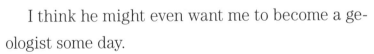

"Pay attention, son," my father tells me, scowling. "I'm bringing up this unpleasant subject for a reason. Ms. Sanchez called to say you were bothering your neighbor in class this afternoon."

"Ms. Sanchez *tattled* on me?" I ask.

I am really, really mad at my teacher when I hear this, because you can get in trouble at school for something, and you can get in trouble at home, but you should never get in trouble both places for the same thing.

I think it's a rule.

It ought to be!

Also, Ms. Sanchez never calls my parents on the days when I'm good. So it's not fair *twice*.

"Ms. Sanchez and your mother and I decided to hold regular telephone conferences, ever since your progress report," my dad tells me. "We want to handle problems as each one arises."

"Well, what about if my neighbor *wanted* to be bothered, did you ever think about that?" I ask, angry enough to talk back to my dad. This is never a good idea, even on a good day.

Which this is not.

"Manners," Dad says, almost growling the word.

But my neighbor in class is Annie Pat Master-

son, I want to explain, and she loves it when I make her laugh in class! She's bored, that's why.

"Make that face again," she whispers, and so I do—just to be polite.

But does anyone except Annie Pat thank me? **NO!**

My dad is telling me something else. "And Ms. Sanchez said that you teased Emma McGraw during Spanish, when she tried to say '*arroz con pollo*,'" he says, continuing his invisible list of *Things That My Son EllRay Has Done Wrong.*

He pronounces it right, of course: "*Ah-rose cone POY-yoh.*"

"The way Emma said it was funny," I object, remembering how mad she looked when she kept saying "*polo*" by accident.

And I kept saying "Marco!" like in the swimming pool game. "*Marco! Polo! Marco! Polo!*"

It made me feel good when everyone laughed, even Emma, and it kind of erased the memory of Jared and Stanley grinding my ribs and giving me "two for flinching" at recess.

That's why I did it.

"But listen, son," my dad says, leaning forward. "You cannot joke around if it's going to disrupt the class. The good of the class always comes first."

He's a teacher, so of course he thinks that.

"I know," I mumble.

"But it will be hard to change the way you behave at school," my father says. "So I'm going to make it interesting for you, son."

I look at him and wonder what he is up to. "Interesting, like how?" I ask.

"Interesting, like Disneyland, next Saturday,"

he tells me, smiling. He loosens his tie—yes, my father almost always wears a tie—as if he's about to get on a ride this very minute.

Disneyland!

We went once with relatives, when I was four, and then we tried to go again two years ago, but my little sister got an earache during the drive to Anaheim, which ruined everything. We had to turn around and drive back home, and my dad has been too busy to go again since.

But added to my father's busyness is the fact that he is not the type of person who likes to have fun. Not *regular people* fun.

"Do you think you can keep your nose clean for an entire week, EllRay?" my dad asks. "With no more bad news during telephone conferences?"

"*Keeping my nose clean*" means not messing up.

"Mmm-hmm," I say, nodding. I am pinching my lips together in case I accidentally say something that needs improvement. I don't want my dad to change his mind—because I really, really, really want to go to Disneyland.

I am already choosing what ride I want to go on first. Alfie can go on the baby rides, but I want to go on the scary ones.

I *sort of* want to, anyway.

"Mmm-hmm," I say again, humming my agreement.

Dad laughs. "Well, okay, then," he says, rubbing my head with the flat of his big hand. "We'll see if you can behave well at school the rest of this week. And that will be the new EllRay Jakes from now on."

The new EllRay Jakes. I guess he's tired of the old one.

But I have a feeling Jared and Stanley will probably hate me even more if I act perfect for a whole week. *Then* what will happen?

BOP, BOP, BOP! Or **GRIND, GRIND, GRIND**.

And then I'll lose my temper, and Ms. Sanchez will find out, and she'll tattle to my parents, and bye-bye Disneyland.

I cannot let that happen.

✳ **4** ✳

WHO'S THE BOSS?

"Play dolls with me, *EllWay*," my little sister says a few minutes later, popping her head out of her room as I walk down the hall. She pronounces some words a little bit wrong, but that's okay, because she's only four years old.

"No way, Alfie," I say. "But me and my video game will keep you company." And I go get *Die, Creature, Die*, which my mom thinks is too violent, but it's not.

Last summer, when I was still trying to be nice about playing dolls, mostly to keep Alfie out of my room, a doll head came off in my hand for no reason, and she freaked, like I'd done it on purpose. And I was just trying to be nice.

So, no more playing dolls.

Alfie is very cute. Everyone says so, especially her, but she probably only says that because she

hears it so much. She is golden brown like an acorn, and she wears her hair in three little puffy braids with matching hair-things on the ends. One braid is on top of her head, and there is one on each side.

I can't really describe girls' hair right.

The only trouble with Alfie is the same thing that is the trouble with me: our names. See, "EllRay" is short for "L-period-Ray," which is short for "Lancelot Raymond." And "Alfie" is short for "Alfleta," which means "beautiful elf" in some language from the olden days. Saxon, I think Mom said.

My mom wants to be a fantasy writer some day, that's why we got such goofy names.

My dad should have told her no. Not about wanting to be a writer, of course, but about the names. It's too late now, though.

We have to live with these names *forever.*

"I'm back," I tell Alfie, who is sitting on her rug. She has just finished piling up a stack of doll clothes.

"Which is cuter?" she asks, holding up two little dresses.

"I dunno," I say, trying to settle into my game. "The red one, I guess."

"Okay," she says, and she starts putting the yellow dress on her bare-naked doll.

"How come you even asked me which one is cuter?" I say, feeling a little mad at her, even though I don't really care about the dresses, of course. "So you could do the exact opposite?"

"Nuh-uh," Alfie says, shaking her head as she tries to cram her doll's skinny arm through a sleeve. "I just like to hear you talk, that's all."

"Oh," I say, feeling a little better.

"Because nobody talks to me at day care anymore," she says sadly.

"Oh, c'mon, Alfie. That's not true," I tell her—because if there's one thing about my little sister, it's that she has a lot of friends.

Friends are very important to girls, I have noticed. They even keep score about them: how many they have, what their ranking is. Friends are like a girl's very own personal sports team.

It's different for boys, or at least for me. Sure, I want to have at least one or two friends so there will be someone to hang out with and watch my back, especially lately, but I don't get all bent out of shape about it.

"Suzette told the other girls not to talk to me," Alfie says, still looking down at her doll.

Suzette is this bossy little girl in my sister's day care who likes to keep all the other little girls scared about whether or not she likes them. Big deal.

"She told *everyone* that?" I ask, hating Suzette for one hot second.

"Well, she told Maya and Joelle not to," Alfie tells me. "And Suzette's the boss of our day care, so that's that."

"Aren't your teachers the boss of day care?" I ask her. "I think you should tell them what Suzette is doing, Alfie, and then maybe she'd stop."

"But she might think of something worse," Alfie says, picking up two little doll jackets. "Which one is cuter?" she asks me.

The blue one is cuter, but I don't tell Alfie that. "The orange one," I say, and sure enough, she starts putting the blue one one her doll.

I smile and start playing my handheld video game again.

"Who's the boss of the world?" Alfie asks me, holding her doll up to admire it.

I sigh and press Pause. "No one, I guess," I tell her. "I mean, the world is all divided up, and there are different bosses for different places.

The little places, too. Even Oak Glen has a boss, you know."

"Huh," Alfie says, not asking who that boss is—which is a good thing, because I don't know his or her name. I don't get to vote yet, that's why. "Well," she asks after a couple of minutes, "who's the boss of our family, at least? I vote for Mommy."

And I can't help but laugh, this is such a crazy conversation. "Why not Dad?" I ask her.

"Because whenever we go to Target and Mommy wants something, Daddy says, 'You're the boss, Louise.'"

"I think he's just kidding," I tell her.

"So *Daddy's* the boss?" Alfie asks me.

"No," I say. "I mean, they're both the boss of *us*. Not of each other, I don't think."

"But you're not the boss of me, EllWay," Alfie says, scowling.

"That's okay," I tell her. "Because I don't even *wanna* be the boss of you. It'd be too much work."

Alfie thinks about this for a minute. "Well," she finally asks, "who's the boss of the third grade at school? In your class? Not counting your teacher."

"No one," I say, snapping out the words. But a picture of Jared's head has floated into my imagination like a big ugly balloon.

"There's a boy boss and a girl boss, right?" Alfie asks, trying to work it out.

"Nobody's the boss," I repeat. "But I guess Jared Matthews is the meanest boy, and Cynthia Harbison is the meanest girl."

"Then I hate them," Alfie says, as loyal to me as I am to her.

"You don't have to hate them," I tell her. "But you're lucky you don't have to go to school with them, that's for sure."

Alfie plays in silence for a few quiet minutes, just long enough for me to get into my game once more. Then, sure enough, she thinks of something else to say. "But if Jared and Cynthia moved away," she says, "and so did Suzette, there'd probably just be someone else being the meanest. Or the bossiest."

I look up just long enough to mess up my score.

"I guess you're right," I say, surprised that she could figure something like this out all by herself.

"'Course I'm right, EllWay," she tells me. "Because there can't just be three holes in the world where those mean kids used to be."

"I guess not," I say, giving up and turning off my game.

Sometimes, when I talk to Alfie, I feel like I'm on a merry-go-round that just keeps spinning, no matter how much I want to get off. "I'm gonna go to bed," I tell my spacey little sister. "I think I'm getting a headache."

"Try sleeping with your feet on the pillow," she calls after me. "Because maybe then your headache will get mixed up and go someplace else!"

Let's hope she doesn't want to be a doctor when she grows up, that's all.

✳ **5** ✳

GLOM

"You were almost late," Annie Pat whispers as I slide into my seat on Tuesday morning. Her red pigtails shine like two orange highway cones.

"I was *almost* late, but I'm *not* late. There's a big difference," I inform Annie Pat, just as Ms. Sanchez begins to take roll.

Annie Pat blinks her dark blue eyes once and looks confused. She can usually count on me to make at least one goofy face or blarty noise first thing in the morning.

Not this week, though.

See, I have a plan, and this morning I timed things just right.

What I did was this: I sneaked into school early, and then I washed my hands for ten minutes in the boys' bathroom so I wouldn't see Jared or Stanley.

It wasn't because I am scared of them, though. I'm just being careful.

My plan is to avoid trouble *all week long* by doing something else or being someplace else whenever Jared or Stanley comes looking for me. But it's just for this week.

Ms. Sanchez starts announcing stuff, as usual, and I start daydreaming, as usual. But now I have something exciting to daydream about. Disneyland!

And today, **TUESDAY**, the world—or at least Ms. Sanchez's third grade class at Oak Glen Primary School in Oak Glen, California—is going to see me, EllRay Jakes, being a perfect kid.

"Pay attention, Mr. Jakes," Ms. Sanchez says, sounding tired already—and it's not even nine o'clock in the morning.

✕ ✕ ✕

"Hurry up, EllRay, or all the kickballs will be gone," Corey calls out, speeding past me on his way out the door for nutrition break, which is recess with healthy snacks, basically. At least they're *supposed* to be healthy.

"Yeah," Kevin calls over his shoulder. He is moving as fast as a person can humanly move without actually running, because there is *No Running* in the halls at Oak Glen Primary School.

And that is only one of our school's many, many rules.

I sneak out the door while Jared and Stanley

are still getting their snacks out of their grubby backpacks. Jared and Stanley love nutrition break because they love eating, but Corey, Kevin, and I usually eat our snacks—and some of our lunch, too—*before* school, so we'll have more time to play.

And—I'm out the door, and I'm free!

Now, the trick will be to glom onto a group of kids so Jared and Stanley can't yank me aside and grind my ribs, hoist my pants hurting-high, or knuckle my hair.

And I'll have to do the same sneaking away and glomming at lunch, too.

And at recess.

And after school. For three more days.

Glomming is going to take all my attention. I sure hope Ms. Sanchez doesn't expect me to learn anything new this week!

✻ **6** ✻

BUK, BUK, BUK

"Ooo," Jared whispers at lunch. "Here he is, *finally*. What's the matter, EllRay? Scared to be alone with us?"

"Yeah," Stanley chimes in, his voice soft. "***BUK, BUK, BUK!***"

This is his idea of how a chicken talks, I guess, which is just dumb, because chickens do not talk. But basically, Stanley is saying that I'm chicken.

"Shut up," I tell him out of the side of my mouth.

I suddenly realize, though, that I am sitting at the end of the picnic table bench, not somewhere safe in the middle—like between Corey and Kevin, for example. Or even between two girls, if girls sat at our table—which they don't, lately, ever since the food fight.

But that's a whole different story.

Uh-oh. I have made a b-i-i-i-g mistake.

Jared makes a knuckly fist and secretly starts twisting it into my ribs, which are still aching from yesterday's knuckle-grinding. He smiles at everyone else in a fake-friendly way while he is doing it, so they won't know something bad is happening.

Stanley stands back and watches the knuckling, and his eyes are nervous and bright behind his smudged glasses. They look even more lizard-like than usual.

Every single rib I have on that side burns, and I try not to cringe, but I can feel myself starting to get mad.

Okay. When I lose my temper, three things happen:

1. First, I can feel all the juices inside my body start racing around really fast.
2. Then my heart starts pounding so hard I can barely hear people talk.
3. And then my hands get clenchy.

Orange sparks may fly out of my ears, for all I know!

Seated across from me, Kevin does not know why I am leaning over so far. "Hey, EllRay, you're going to fall," he says, giving me a friendly smile. Then he goes back to eating his sandwich, a gigantic grinder with pink flaps of meat hanging out. Kevin's hand grips the roll as if it might try to escape from him at any moment.

It would if it could!

"Yeah. Stop crowding, EllRay," Jared tells me, giving me an extra-hard knuckle twist.

"*Yowtch!* Quit it, Jared," I yell.

"'*Quit it, Jared*,'" Stanley says in a whiny voice, trying to copy me—even though I didn't really whine. Like I said, I yelled. In a manly way.

I try to count to ten, which is what my mom says to do when I start getting mad. *One, two, three, four.* My lips move a little as I silently run through the numbers.

"Oh, look. He's gonna cry. The widdle baby's sad," Jared says, sounding happy. Then he throws back his head and gives his famous **HAW−HAW− HAW** laugh.

"I'm not crying," I say, trying to get to my feet.

I do not want to get into trouble, even at lunch, because the lunch monitor would tell Ms. Sanchez. Then Ms. Sanchez would call my parents, and bye-bye Disneyland on Saturday.

But do I want to go through the rest of my life saying, "***BUK, BUK, BUK***"?

No way!

❈ 7 ❈

IT'S DIFFERENT WITH MY MOM

My mom thinks there is always a reason when people—especially kids—are mean, but even though I am only eight years old, I know better.

I think some people—*especially* kids—are mean for no reason.

What about when a mean person shoves someone in the hall? Or "accidentally" knocks the back of that person's head when he is drinking at the water fountain? Or grabs his lunch and plays keep-away with it?

That person does it because he can.

But I don't tell my mom that, because it would only make her sad. Even though she likes to write books about pretend-wonderful things that could have happened in a long-ago time, in real life she is a little bit of a worrywart when it comes to Alfie and me. She wants us never to get hurt.

Just as I think this thought, Mom pops her head around the door to my bedroom. "Can I tuck you in, EllRay?" she asks, smiling.

"Sure," I tell her, scooching over in bed to make room for her to sit next to me. "Good," my mom

says, settling in for a before-bedtime visit, which is secretly one of my favorite things, because:

1. It's not like when I'm at school, where I can never really relax because I don't know what's gonna happen next.
2. And it's not like when I'm with Alfie, where I always have to watch her to make sure she doesn't try to fly down the stairs or something crazy like that.
3. And it's not like when I'm with my dad, where he is either trying to keep me from messing up in the future or scolding me for messing up in the past. Sometimes I think I must be a disappointment to him, he is so important and smart. And strong. And tall.

It's different with my mom. My mom is usually a very relaxing person, and she likes me no matter what. She even likes the *old* EllRay Jakes.

"Your daddy told me about your Disneyland deal," Mom says, arranging my covers more neatly under my chin. "I guess you're pretty happy about that, hmm?"

"Yeah," I say. "If I don't mess it up for everyone.

Don't tell Alfie about it yet, okay? Just in case."

"Okay," Mom promises. "But I know you can do it, honey bun."

"It's—it's kind of like a bribe, though, isn't it?" I ask. "Us getting to go to Disneyland, but only if I'm good. And I thought you guys said that bribing people was wrong. Even bribing *kids*."

My mom laughs a little. "I might have handled things differently," she says quietly. "But whatever works, EllRay—because I want everyone at Oak Glen Primary School to see the same wonderful boy I see whenever I look at you."

"I'm not *always* wonderful," I admit in the dark.

"To me you are," Mom says. "Deep down inside. But—what's going on?"

"Like, in the *world*?" I ask, pretending I don't know what she means.

"Not in *the* world," she says. "Just in *your* world."

"My world's fine," I lie.

But it's the kind of lie that is meant to keep someone from feeling bad, like if a person asks, "*How does my new haircut look?*" and you say,

"Perfectly normal," instead of *"Like somebody went after you with broken kindergarten scissors."*

"Oh, come on," Mom says in her softest voice. "I know you better than that, EllRay Jakes. And something is troubling you. Is it your progress report?"

"Yeah, it's that," I say, taking the easy way out—because she offered it to me.

Mom leans over to kiss my on my forehead, which is all wrinkled from fibbing. "Well, I wouldn't worry too much," she tells me. "Time passes, doesn't it? I'll bet your work has already improved since Ms. Sanchez wrote that report."

"But it's hard," I say, telling the truth for the first time since she sat down.

"What's hard?" Mom asks.

"Paying attention in class," I tell her. "And remembering all the rules. And sitting in my chair without wiggling. And not bothering my neighbor, even when she wants to be bothered. And not getting mad on the playground. It's hard just being *me*, Mom."

"Oh, EllRay, I know it is," she says, scooping me

into a hug. "But like I said before, being you is also a wonderful thing, honey bun."

"Not so far it isn't," I try to say, but my mouth is smooshed against her sweater and she probably doesn't even hear me.

Mom kisses me on my forehead again and pulls the covers up to my chin. "Well, nighty-night," she says, as if every problem in every world, not just mine, has now been solved. "Close your eyes and go to sleep," she tells me. "Because tomorrow's going to be a beautiful day, EllRay."

✕　✕　✕

Today has been a nervous Tuesday for me, I think, lying in the dark, especially because of what happened at lunch. But Mom has made it better, somehow. And I did make it through the afternoon without getting twisted, pounded, or whomped again.

So that's been one whole day without getting into trouble.

Maybe Mom is right. Maybe I can do it!

✳ **8** ✳

MS. SANCHEZ SAYS

"Quiet, ladies and gentlemen," Ms. Sanchez says on **WEDNESDAY** morning from the front of the class, and she taps her solid-gold pen on her desk.

We all try to look as if we are paying attention, even though half of the class feels like falling asleep because the room is so hot, and the other half—the half with me in it—wants to run outside and play.

It is a beautiful day, just the way Mom said it would be.

"Pay attention, please," Ms. Sanchez says, tapping her pen again. "I have an announcement. We're going to do a science experiment. It's Mudshake Day!"

"But I thought we only had to do science on Tuesdays," Heather Patton says in a really loud whisper, because you're not supposed to talk out loud in class without raising your hand first.

Heather sits behind me in class, and ever since her teenage sister told her she was going to have to cut up a dead frog in science class when she is a teenager, she has hated the entire subject.

Heather doesn't even like frogs that are *alive*, much less dead.

I am not exactly looking forward to cutting up a dead frog, by the way, but it might be interesting—*if* the frog didn't get run over, and *if* it died of old age after leading a long and happy life. For a frog.

"From now on, Heather," Ms. Sanchez says with an ice cube in her voice, "please raise your hand if you have something to say."

"Sorry," Heather mumbles.

"With this experiment," Ms. Sanchez says, sneaking a look at her notes, "we will continue our exploration of soil and its components."

Okay. "Components" means "parts," I happen

to know, only Ms. Sanchez can't just say "parts," for some reason. Probably because it's too simple a word, and we wouldn't get smart if she always said things the simplest way.

So Ms. Sanchez has to say "soil" when she really means "dirt," for example.

Next to me, Annie Pat Masterson aims a smile at Emma McGraw, because they both love science, even when it's just about dirt.

"Here is what your ideal garden soil is made up of," Ms. Sanchez says, and she writes something on the board:

1. 40% SAND
2. 40% SILT
3. 20% CLAY

"Now, who can tell me what this means?" she asks.

Cynthia raises her hand and starts talking before Ms. Sanchez even calls on her, which is typical of Cynthia. "'Ideal' means 'best,'" she says in a very loud voice, and she smiles, using all her teeth, and looks around like she is waiting for us to cheer.

Ms. Sanchez sighs. "That is correct, Cynthia."

she says. "But I was really talking about what the numbers on the board mean."

"Well, *I* didn't know that," Cynthia says, folding her arms across her chest and frowning, which is never a good sign with her.

Cynthia is a girl who knows how to hold a grudge.

The whole class sits in silence for a minute, hoping someone will raise their—her—hand.

In other words, we are counting on Kry Rodriguez to save us.

Kry's real name is Krysten, and she is pretty, with long black hair, and she moved to Oak Glen just before Thanksgiving, and she is very good at math. She slowly raises her hand like there is a red balloon tied to her wrist.

"Yes, Kry?" Ms. Sanchez says, smiling in relief.

Kry clears her throat. "I think the numbers mean that *almost* half of the soil is sand," she says, "and *almost* half is silt, and half of almost-half is clay. Which adds up to one hundred percent."

"Big deal," Cynthia coughs-says into her hand.

Heather laughs to back her up. "Whatever silt is," she mutters.

"And what is silt?" Ms. Sanchez asks in her coldest voice. "Heather? Perhaps you can enlighten us."

"Enlighten" sounds like Ms. Sanchez wants Heather to make us all turn white, which most of my class already is, basically, except for me, Kevin, and two very quiet girls who go to the same church, not mine.

Or else it sounds like our teacher wants Heather to make us light as feathers so we could float up to the ceiling, which would be cool, but no such luck. That's not what Ms. Sanchez means. What "enlighten us" really means is to shine a light on something, only a pretend light, not a real light. In other words, she wants Heather to explain to us what silt is.

I know this, but I do not raise my hand. I don't want to make Jared and Stanley any madder at me than they already are, which they will be if they think I'm showing off by acting smart in class.

"I don't know," Heather mumbles again.

"Anyone?" Ms. Sanchez asks, but no one raises their hand. Not even Kry.

Ms. Sanchez starts to pull her big blue dictionary from the shelf. *"Look it up!"* she usually says when a strange word comes along.

Like every minute, practically.

But all of a sudden, Fiona McNulty slowly raises her hand. This is something that she hardly ever does, because she is the shyest kid in class.

"Yes, Fiona?" Ms. Sanchez says, trying to hide her surprise.

Fiona closes her eyes before she speaks, as if she is about to get a shot at the doctor's office. "Silt is like this teeny tiny dirt that the water moves around, and when the water goes away, the tiny dirt kind of piles up all over the place," she says, squeaking out the words. "My grandpa lives near the Colorado River," she adds, opening one eye as she explains how she knows such an unusual thing.

"Well, that's basically correct," Ms. Sanchez says, after checking her notes once more. "Very good, Fiona."

Fiona blushes.

"And so here is our experiment, people," Ms. Sanchez says. "We have eight glass jars with lids, filled up almost to the top with water, and we have eight mystery soil samples to work with."

Teachers always use words like "mystery" when

they are trying to make something boring sound interesting.

"But—there are twenty-four kids in our class," Cynthia objects, looking around.

"So how many students will be on each mud-shake team?" Ms. Sanchez asks, peeking at her watch. "Tick-tock, people."

"Tick-tock" means "hurry up," when she says it like this.

We all look at Kry. "Three," she says.

"Correct," Ms. Sanchez tells us. "So listen as I call out the teams."

✕   ✕   ✕

"Emma, Jared, and EllRay," she finally says.

Well, it could have been worse, I remind myself. It could have been Stanley, Jared, and EllRay.

"I want each team to carefully pour its mystery soil sample into its water jar," Ms. Sanchez calls out, still reading from her notes.

We let Emma do the pouring, of course, because she's a girl, and girls are always neat. Neater than boys, anyway.

"Now," Ms. Sanchez says, "I am going to come around and add a spoonful of alum to each jar before you start shaking it."

"*AL-um*," she pronounces it.

Across the room, Annie Pat raises her hand. "Why?" she asks. "What's alum?"

Like I said before, Annie Pat and Emma love science, and they are always full of questions whenever our class does something the least bit scientific.

But that's okay, because it uses up the time.

Ms. Sanchez sighs, as if she was afraid Annie Pat or Emma would ask this question. "Alum has something to do with aluminum," she says. "And for some reason, it makes the soil samples separate more easily into their varying layers of sand, silt, and clay, which will help our experiment. But I'd appreciate it if you'd look up '*alum*' for us tonight, Annie Pat, and fill us all in first thing tomorrow morning."

"Okay," Annie Pat tells her, looking important as she writes down her own personal assignment.

Ms. Sanchez adds a spoonful of white stuff— alum—to each glass jar. "Now stir," she tells us, and Emma hands me the Popsicle stick as if stirring things up is obviously my kind of job. So I do it, because who cares?

"Lids on," Ms. Sanchez says, "and shake!"

That's going to be *Jared's* job, of course. Jared the mighty, Jared the strong.

In about two seconds, he crams the lid on the jar wrong, turns toward me, and starts shaking the mud-filled jar hard, hard, hard.

He practically aims it at me.

Without holding down the lid.

And—**FLOOIE!** There is mud—components of soil, I mean—all over my best, almost-new T-shirt

that has a San Diego Padres logo on it and everything. San Diego is the largest city near Oak Glen.

It is the very same T-shirt I was supposed to wear to the Sycamore Shopping Center this afternoon with my little sister Alfie and my mom, who was going to buy me a corn dog because I got almost all of my Monday spelling words right, for once.

It is the T-shirt Jared looks at with hungry eyes whenever I wear it.

"Oh, no!" Emma cries, holding her cheeks with both hands like the kid in that old movie.

"Oops," Jared says, with the happiest look in the world on his big dumb face. "Sorry, EllRay."

And it's only Wednesday *morning.*

✳ **9** ✳

WHACKED ON WEDNESDAY

It is now noon, and even though the top half of me is covered with mud, or—excuse me—*soil*, I have made it almost halfway through the week without getting into trouble.

Disneyland, here I come! *Maybe.*

"Did Jared throw mud at you this morning on purpose?" Kevin McKinley asks me.

"Huh?" I say. We are the only ones sitting at the third grade boys' lunch table so far. When the bell rang, I ran outside fast, so I could finish my lunch early and then go wash my hands for half an hour.

I guess Kevin was just hungry.

Kevin takes a big bite

of his big sandwich, chews slowly, swallows the bite, and then takes a long swig of his chocolate milk without even using a straw.

Milk dribbles down my shirt whenever I try that, but I guess today it wouldn't make much of a difference.

Kevin clears his throat. "Corey said that Emma told him it looked like Jared threw that mud on you on purpose during the experiment," he says, and he gets ready to take another bite of his sandwich.

Wow! I didn't know news traveled so fast around here. Or that boys listened to girls. "Why would Jared do that?" I ask, not really answering Kevin's question.

"'Cause he's mean?" Kevin guesses, his mouth full again.

Corey slides onto the bench. "Who's mean?" he asks, opening his lunch sack and peering eagerly into it—even though he's already eaten half of what was inside. All that's probably left is a sack of carrot sticks and the same box of raisins his mom keeps packing every day, even though Corey never eats them.

Those raisins are practically *antiques.*

But don't worry, we'll share our food with him.

"News flash. Jared's mean," Kevin says, filling him in.

"Duh," Corey says, making a face. "Emma says she thought you were going to sock Jared right in the mouth this morning, EllRay."

"Only he's so short he couldn't *reach* my mouth," Jared said, flinging himself so hard onto the bench on the other side of the table that everything shakes: table, benches, antique raisins, little sacks of carrot sticks, us. "EllRay socking me," he sneers in a loud voice. "Like that's gonna happen. Right, Stanley?"

"Right," Stanley says, sliding in next to him.

"You sound kind of like a robot, Stanley," Kevin says thoughtfully, after taking another slurp of his chocolate milk.

Everyone at the table—even Jared and Stanley—is quiet for a second, because Kevin is nearly as big as Jared, so what does that mean in terms of a possible fight? And Kevin is one of those guys who almost never gets mad, but when he does, watch out.

"You got a problem with me, McKinley?" Jared finally asks, because everyone is waiting for him to say *something.*

"Not yet," Kevin says calmly, and he takes another bite of his sandwich.

I wish I could say something like that. Maybe if I was bigger, a *lot* bigger, like half a person bigger, I could.

This talk between Kevin and Jared was almost worth sticking around to hear, but my plan to avoid getting whacked on Wednesday has now been ruined—because I'm sitting here with Jared Matthews and Stanley Washington instead of being in the bathroom washing my hands, and Kevin McKinley can't be *everywhere*, not for the whole rest of the day.

Or the two school days left in the week.

"Oops," Jared says, and then—*after* he says "*Oops*"—he knocks his open carton of milk in my direction. The milk splashes on my peanut butter sandwich and floods the table. It creeps toward the edge of the table—where it will look like I wet my pants if it dribbles onto my lap.

And so even though I don't want to, I scramble to my feet to get out of its way.

"Look at EllRay run," Jared says, laughing, even though I haven't run anywhere—*yet*.

Everyone waits for me to say something or do something to get even with Jared, but I just clamp my mouth shut and think about Disneyland.

It better be worth it.

"***BUK, BUK, BUK,***" Jared murmurs softly, but loud enough for everyone to hear.

"Dude, you owe him lunch," Kevin says, and **SWOOP!** He grabs the sandwich from Jared's big square paw and hands it over to me.

"Oops," I say, and then I drop Jared's sandwich on the ground, and I stomp on it. "Sorry, Jared," I tell him, not sounding sorry at all.

Jared is halfway to his feet, looking really, really mad, and also hungry, but there is no way he can complain without looking dumb in front of everyone, including a few girls—Emma, Heather, and Annie Pat—who are watching us from a nearby table with worried eyes.

After all, Jared made a "mistake," spilling his milk, and I made a "mistake," dropping the sandwich on the ground and stomping on it, so we're even, right?

But I know that somehow, somewhere, I'm going to have to pay *double* for this.

I just hope it's not until next week, that's all.

✳ **10** ✳

THUMPED ON THURSDAY

"Why is Jared so mad at you?" Emma asks me just before I am probably about to get thumped on **THURSDAY**, because of the sandwich thing the day before.

It is eight fifteen, and school hasn't even started yet.

"He's not mad," I tell her. "I don't know."

That is two different answers to the same question, but Emma can handle it. "Why don't you have a meeting with him and find out?" she suggests.

This is a very embarrassing conversation.

Also, boys do not solve their problems by having meetings. That's much more a a girl thing, in my opinion. And all of a sudden, I can feel my juices racing, my heart pounding, and my hands getting clenchy.

In other words, I am about to lose my temper—with Emma!

"Well, why don't you have a meeting with your mom to find out why your *hair* is so curly?" I ask, even though I like curly hair.

Especially Emma's, which is long and brown and tangly and always smells good. I don't know how girls do that.

Emma touches her hair, and her eyes get wide, and she steps back, surprised. "Don't get mad at *me*," she says in a shaky voice. "I was only trying to help, that's all."

"Well, stop trying," I tell her, turning to walk away—because it's time to go wash my hands for a while, and *nobody* can help me.

Especially not a girl.

✕ ✕ ✕

It is now just after lunch, and I am on my way to the front of the class to talk about the three layers of soil in our experiment jars.

But Ms. Sanchez turns her back to the class for a second—and I land flat on my face on the floor.

FWUMP.

It's because I had to walk past Jared, that's why. He tripped me!

Okay. There are three things you can do when you fall flat on your face in front of the whole class:

1. You can pretend you are dead, or at least unconscious. But then your teacher will call the nurse, the principal, and your parents.

2. You can pretend it was a joke, and you meant to fall flat on your face. Only it's hard to do that when you think you might throw up or start crying if you try to talk. And if I start crying in front of the whole class,

Jared's supreme goal will have come true, and I can never let that happen.

3. You can—

"Oh, EllRay, sweetie, are you all right?" Ms. Sanchez asks, racing to my side. I know it's her, because I recognize her shoes.

Ms. Sanchez just called me "sweetie" in front of the whole class.

I will never live this down.

This week just keeps getting more and more terrible!

"*'Sweetie,'*" Kevin whispers, cackling. This will be my nickname from now on, I just know it.

"Uh-h-h," I say, which is supposed to mean, *"Sure, I'm fine!"* Only it's hard to explain that from flat on the floor when there isn't any air in your lungs. I try to sit up.

"Jared *tripped* him," Annie Pat cries.

"On purpose," Emma says.

Oh, great! Emma has already forgiven me for

making fun of her hair, and I didn't even apologize yet. Now I feel worse than before.

Thanks a lot, Emma.

"I did not trip him," Jared objects. "I was stretching, that's all, and EllRay got in the way of my foot. *Ow*," he says a little late, rubbing it.

Ms. Sanchez ignores everyone but me. "Are you all right, EllRay?" she asks again, her voice as soft as a mom's.

"I'm fine," I say, struggling to stand up.

After I am on my feet again, I look around the room. Jared is waiting for me to tell on him, but I don't, and he looks confused.

"Do you think you should go see the nurse?" Ms. Sanchez asks me.

"Nuh-uh," I tell her. "I just want to talk about soil and its components, that's all—so I can get credit for doing this very interesting experiment."

"Well, if you're sure," Ms. Sanchez says, still looking worried.

"I'm positive," I tell her, and I hobble the rest of the way to the front of the class.

❇ **11** ❇

BAD VIBES

"I have an announcement to make," a serious-looking Ms. Sanchez says to us later that afternoon, after recess, and we instantly hold still in our seats, because you can never tell. "I've been picking up some bad vibes lately," Ms. Sanchez says, looking hard at us.

We have learned by now that "bad vibes" is her way of saying that something in our class feels wrong to her, but she can't say exactly what.

Hearing this announcement, we all relax a little, because—what else is new? There is always *some* bad vibe floating around our class.

1. Sometimes, one of the girls gets her feelings hurt, or a couple of girls get into their version of a fight, and the whole class suffers. Girls know how

to spread their misery around better than boys, who like to keep things secret.

2. Or sometimes, we hear about something bad that has happened outside of school, in some other kid's family—like someone getting sick, or even someone dying,

which is what happened to Corey's grandma before Christmas. That also makes bad vibes, of course, because deep down we all sort of care about each other. Also, I think we're afraid some of the bad might rub off on us.

3. And when we heard last fall that Ms. Sanchez's dog died, those dead dog vibes made us sad for days. Even kids like me who don't get to have a dog, because Alfie's allergic. Those vibes were the worst of all.

This bad vibe is different, though, because I have a feeling it's about me. But no one except Jared, Stanley, and I knows that—and we're not going to talk.

"Is there anything going on that I should know about?" Ms. Sanchez asks us. "Any problems we should be discussing? Because I wanted our new year to start out right, and it just *isn't*."

Cynthia's hand shoots up, and Ms. Sanchez calls on her. Cynthia stands up. "Well, *I* didn't do anything wrong," she says loudly. "And neither did Heather."

Heather wiggles in her seat and smiles, happy to be included in anything Cynthia has to say.

But Ms. Sanchez frowns. "I didn't say anyone in this class has misbehaved," she says, trying to clear things up. "I was simply stating that things do not feel right around here."

And she looks at each boy in the class one at a time with her superpower vision.

I guess Ms. Sanchez has narrowed down that bad vibe.

Corey Robinson blushes under his freckles.

Kevin McKinley looks like he wants to run out of the room.

Stanley Washington looks down at his desk and starts polishing his glasses like crazy.

Jared Matthews stares straight ahead, his face as stony as one of the pieces of granite on the display shelf in my dad's home office.

And I, EllRay Jakes, feel as though Ms. Sanchez can tell every single thing that has happened with Jared, Stanley, and me just by looking at my face.

But she can't, I keep telling myself. She *can't.*

Ms. Sanchez shakes her head, looking disappointed in us. "You know you can come to me with any problem, don't you?" she says, speaking to everyone in the class this time.

The girls nod, looking very serious, but all the boys just stare at her. Because—who wants to talk about their problems? Not us!

Boys just want their problems to go away, and the sooner the better.

Now Ms. Sanchez sighs. "Well, my door's always

open if anyone has anything they want to share with me," she tells us.

And that's just messed up, because we don't even know where she lives. So what difference does it make whether her door is open or not?

Also, if she means that her door is always open *at school*, that's not true either. The custodian locks every single classroom door at the end of the day.

And if she means that we can come talk to her during recess, that's not true *either*, because she's always in the faculty lounge. If a kid ever tried to walk in there, the world would probably come to an end.

"Does everyone have that straight?" Ms. Sanchez asks us, and we all nod again.

Especially the boys this time.

Especially Jared, Stanley, and me.

"Good," Ms. Sanchez tells us, not sounding like it's good at all. "I guess you'd better gather your things," she says, "because the buzzer is about to sound. And let's all start out fresh on Friday, shall we?"

And we nod for the third time, except for Cynthia,

who says, "We shall! Especially me and Heather!"

You can always count on Cynthia to get the last word.

Only she doesn't, this time.

"It's '*Heather and me*,' Miss Harbison," Ms. Sanchez says, sounding tired, tired, tired.

But I feel pretty excited, because—only one more day to go!

✷ **12** ✷

NOT THAT!

"So, Alfie," my dad says at dinner that night as he helps himself to some rice. "Give us your report."

See, our family has this dinner tradition my mom and dad call "civilized conversation," where each person says the best and worst thing that happened to them that day.

Of course, I have not been telling the truth about my worst things ever since Jared and Stanley started picking on me for no reason a couple of weeks ago.

Alfie twiddles one of her braids, thinking. "Well, my good things are that Suzette wants to be my friend again, and I painted a beautiful picture about a flower," she finally announces.

Suzette is that bossy little girl in my sister's day care, remember?

"You're supposed to choose just one good thing," I tell Alfie, because rules are rules.

And what is the point of a tradition if you do the rules wrong?

"I can choose two things if I want," she tells me, scowling. "Are you saying my beautiful flower picture isn't good?"

"No, he's not saying that, Alfie," my mom says in her *calm-down* voice. "What was your worst thing, honey?"

Alfie scowls, which makes her look like an angry kitten. This is probably not the effect she was hoping for. "My worst thing was when my brother was mean to me at dinner," she tells us.

"All right, then," my dad says. "Moving right along. What about you, Louise?"

It's no fair that my mom and dad have normal names like Louise and Warren when my sister and I get stuck with Alfleta and Lancelot Raymond.

Mom pats her lips with her napkin and looks up at the ceiling. "My good news is that I got a nice rejection letter today for that book I wrote about the enchanted princess who lives in the undersea kingdom," she tells us.

Okay. Now that is just sad, because "rejection" means "no," no matter how good you try to make it sound.

I feel like punching those rejection guys in the nose for insulting my mom!

But instead, I eat another bite of chicken and stare hard at my plate, because one of our rules is that you can't argue about another person's good and bad.

"What did the letter say?" my dad asks.

"That they wanted to see more of my work in the future," Mom tells him, smiling. She looks shy but proud. "And my bad news is that I left the ice cream out on the counter by accident when I got home from the store," she confesses.

There goes dessert, which is bad news for everyone.

"And what about you, son?" Dad asks.

Did I mention that he is still wearing his tie, even though it's just us?

I have been silently rehearsing my answer for the last ten minutes. "My best thing is that I told about the layers of soil in the experiment without messing up," I report. "And the worst—"

"What *about* the layers of soil?" Dad asks, leaning forward as if this is the most interesting thing he has heard all night—which it probably is, because he likes rocks and crystals and minerals better than anything in the world, except us.

"Well," I say, trying hard to remember, "one jar had lots of sand in it, and Ms. Sanchez said that sample was from the desert. And another jar had mostly silt, and that was from some river. And one jar was the perfect mix of sand and silt and clay, which means you could grow stuff in it, Ms. Sanchez said."

"Excellent, EllRay," Dad tells me, beaming. "And what was the worst thing that happened to you today?"

"I dropped my sandwich at lunch," I lie.

Dad looks at me, and his eyes look extra-big behind his glasses. "And that's it?" he asks. "That is absolutely the worst thing that happened to you today?"

I can feel my ears getting hot. "Yes sir," I lie again.

"Then I need to speak to you after dinner, son," Dad says, his voice changing from curious to serious in one second flat. "In my office."

My mom clears her throat, and Alfie looks at me with big sad eyes, like she's feeling really, really sorry for me.

UH—OH.

✕ ✕ ✕

My father is sitting behind his shiny desk, only now he looks like Dr. Warren Jakes, not Dad.

I close the door behind me and listen to the sound of my heart pounding in my ears.

It's no fair to have bad things happen to you at school *and* at home.

It should be one place—at the very most.

I'm not even sure what I have done wrong that my dad is so mad about. It could be so many things!

1. For instance, I didn't brush my teeth this morning, even though I wet my toothbrush so my mom would think I did.
2. And I pulled my bedspread up over the wrinkled sheet and blanket this morning without really making my bed.
3. And I wore a T-shirt that was in the dirty clothes hamper, because I didn't like any of the shirts that were clean.

"Ms. Sanchez called," my dad says. "Just before dinner."

He waits.

This telephone conference thing has gone *too far*.

And why did she pretend she didn't know who was causing that bad vibe?

"But I didn't behave wrong," I say in a croaky, guilty-sounding voice.

I don't even mention Disneyland, because I don't want to give my dad any ideas about canceling our trip. He is the strict kind of dad who might do that.

"I know," my dad says, frowning. "But Ms. Sanchez told me you fell down in class, and she says Jared Matthews might have tripped you on purpose.

She wasn't sure, because her back was turned."

I hold my breath and don't say a word.

"*Did* he trip you, son?" Dad asks gently. "Is there something going on at Oak Glen that we should know about?"

Okay.

When we moved to Oak Glen three years ago, my mom and dad were a little worried, because there aren't that many other families in this town who are African-American. Just about ten or eleven of them, something like that. And at first, my parents were on the lookout for any little thing that would tell them people had some problem with us. But so far, so good— except sometimes I wish there *were* more black kids at our school, just so it would come out even.

Oh, and Alfie told me once that Suzette at day care keeps wanting to touch her braids. But that's a secret, we decided, because we don't want our dad to freak.

He's very sensitive about stuff like that.

"No, nothing," I mumble. "It's okay."

"Speak up, son," my dad reminds me. "Be proud of what you have to say."

"I *am* proud," I tell him, even though my heart

is thudding so hard you can almost see my T-shirt jump. "But Jared tripped me by accident, Dad. Accidents happen, right? That's where the expression comes from."

Sure, I could get Jared in trouble right now by telling on him.

Sure, I could even say he's picking on me because I'm black.

But it's not that! Jared would have said something if it was. He is not the type of kid to keep things to himself. That much is obvious.

Anyway, there are plenty of other things that could be make him want to pick on me. Like, I'm the shortest kid in class, so I'm the easiest to pick on.

And I get all the laughs, so maybe he's jealous.

In fact, I'm better at just about everything at school—except being big—than Jared is.

Or, like I said before, there could be no reason at all. Just him being bored because Christmas is over.

"And you're really all right?" my dad asks, looking me up and down—which doesn't take very much time at all, for obvious reasons.

I nod my head.

"But—why didn't you mention it to your mom or me, EllRay?" Dad asks. "I just don't understand. I certainly think falling flat on your face in class is a worse thing than dropping your sandwich at lunch."

"But dropping my sandwich meant I was hungry all afternoon," I explain, still lying my head off. "And you're not supposed to argue about another person's good or bad," I remind him, even though I probably shouldn't.

Dad sighs. "Well, you have a point there," he finally admits. "But I want you to promise that you'll tell your mother or me if this problem with Jared continues, okay? Because we want to nip this sort of thing in the bud."

I'm not exactly sure what that expression means, but I get the general idea. "I promise," I tell him, crossing my fingers behind my back.

I don't like lying to my dad, but in this case, it's for his own good.

Also, it's for the good of Disneyland.

I think I'll go on the pirate ride first.

"Can I leave now?" I ask. "Because I have homework to do, and I don't want to get behind."

My father looks at me for one long minute. Behind his glasses, his brown eyes still look troubled. "All right, son," he says slowly. "If you're sure everything is really okay at school."

"It is," I tell him. But I pause with my hand on the doorknob and look back. "Thanks, Dad," I say, because all of a sudden, for the very first time, it occurs to me that it is probably hard for him to be him, just the way it's hard for me to be me. He's so prickly and proud, and then he's got all those rocks to lug around.

Maybe it's hard for him, anyway.

✳ **13** ✳

FWACKED ON FRIDAY

It's **FRIDAY**, and as I walk to school, I realize that I am just about worn out from behaving so well.

I can last one more day, however. And then—
YA-HOO!

But it takes me only a few minutes at school to realize that all the grown-ups at Oak Glen are now on the alert for trouble between Jared and me. I guess word gets around. Ms. Sanchez's word, anyway—or maybe my dad's. Who knows?

Our principal is greeting kids on the front steps of the school, as usual. He is very tall, and he has a beard, and you can see him from far away—so it is usually easy to avoid him.

But not today.

"Morning, EllRay," he calls out in a booming voice over the heads of the hurrying kids, and I freeze on the second step from the top. He wades through the kids until he reaches my side. "How's every little thing?" he asks me.

Little. Is he making fun of me because I'm so short? I don't think so, but I'm not really sure.

"Every little thing is fine," I say, looking w-a-a-a-y up at him.

I am never growing a beard, that's for sure. He probably has to shampoo it, and then maybe even use a hair dryer on it. And what about when he eats? Do potato chip crumbs get caught in all that hair?

"Well, I'm just checking in," the principal says, scanning me up and down again with his eyes to make sure I'm really okay.

"Okay. Bye," I say.

The principal narrows his eyes, gives me a search-ing look, and then turns to say, "Morning!" to some other lucky kid.

And I climb the last step and prepare to get fwacked on Friday.

But maybe I won't get fwacked, I think, allowing myself to hope. Maybe grown-ups being on the alert will save me—for this one last day, at least.

And after today, who cares?

✕   ✕   ✕

"You told," Jared whispers, jamming me up against the BEE CAREFUL! WALK, DON'T RUN! poster with bumblebees on it in the hallway.

"Did not," I tell him, even though his chunky arm with orange freckles on it is pressing hard against my chest.

"Did too," Jared mutters, scowling. "The principal said 'Hi' to me this morning in a weird way."

"I didn't tell," I say again. "Ms. Sanchez guessed, I guess. But I didn't say anything to her, or to my parents, either."

"Hello, boys," the office lady says as she walks by holding a mug of steaming hot coffee. She pauses. "Is everything okay?" she asks, looking at me, not Jared.

"Everything's fine," I tell her. "See?" I whisper to Jared when she finally walks away. "I never told *anyone* that you're mad at me for no reason."

"I do too have a reason, and you know it," Jared tells me.

"I do not know it," I say as the kids bounce around us like bumper cars at the county fair. "I never did anything bad to you. In fact, I try to ignore you every chance I get. I'd be doing it now, if I could."

Jared leans in, his green eyes shining. "Well, what about that time you made me look stupid in front of Heather Patton?" he asks, as if this will prove once and for all how right he is to keep going after me.

"*What* time I made you look stupid?" I ask.

What I am really thinking is that he doesn't need any help from me to look stupid in front of *anyone*. But I decide not to say this, because I'm pretty sure it would only make our troubles worse.

"Right before Christmas," he says, getting mad all over again just thinking about it. "You drew that stupid picture of me and then passed it around. And she saw it. And it was right before my birthday, too, and it kinda hurt my feelings."

This last part about the hurt feelings comes out in a mumble.

Okay.

1. First, I barely even remember drawing that picture, it was so long ago.
2. And second, it was a joke.
3. And third, how was I supposed to know it was almost Jared's birthday? It's not like he invited me to his party or anything!
4. And fourth, I am not a very good artist, so it probably didn't even look like Jared.
5. And fifth, what does Jared care what Heather thinks?

And most important of all, *who knew Jared Matthews had feelings?*

Heather Patton is that girl with the too-tight pony-tail, in case you forgot. The girl who hangs around with Cynthia, that clean girl I was telling you about.

"I'm sorry if I hurt your feelings," I tell him, actually meaning it—but only a little.

"Shut up about my feelings, dude!" he bellows, forgetting for a second to be quiet, he is so mad.

"What else can I say?" I ask him, shrugging, even though my heart is pounding.

"Nothing," he says, easing off a little as he sees the principal coming toward us down the hall in that fast walk grown-ups do when they don't want to look silly by running.

"Okay, then," I say in a hurry.

"I won't touch you during school today, *tattletale EllRay*," Jared whispers, "but you better meet me in Pennypacker Park right after school, if you know what's good for you. So I can beat you up."

Only Jared could say something like this and think it makes sense, because why would someone know what's good for them *and* want to get beat up?

But you know what? I think I'm going to do it.

I'll go.

And I'm going to **FIGHT BACK!**

Because then, the whole trouble between Jared Matthews and me will be over with once and for all, and we can start living our normal lives again—whatever those lives were like. I can barely remember.

And even if someone catches us fighting, my dad can't yank Disneyland away from me, because *the fight won't be in school.*

It's going to be *after* school

I will have kept my part of the bargain.

✳ **14** ✳

EUSTACE B. PENNYPACKER MEMORIAL PARK

I don't know who Eustace B. Pennypacker is, or was, but he has a terrible park. It's mostly just boring green grass with clover and bees, and a bunch of trees.

You'd think he could have thrown in a playground while he was at it, but **NO**.

That is why, even though this park is only a block away from our school, kids hardly ever hang out there.

It is probably also why Jared chose the park for our final fight.

No one will see us, and no one will ever find out what happened the afternoon before EllRay Jakes went to Disneyland, sore—but *happy*.

No one except Jared's loyal friend and robot Stanley Washington.

Oops. I forgot about him.

That's okay, though, because even if Stanley takes a swing at me too, I'll be getting whomped so hard by Jared that I probably won't even notice.

And at least I'll be fighting back!

I am sick of looking over my shoulder and washing my hands all the time.

I have gone all day long without telling anyone what is going to happen, because I am *not* a tattletale, no matter what Jared thinks.

Also, it wouldn't do any good, because this fight is between Jared and me—and Stanley, probably, but there's nothing I can do about that.

Jared needs to get even with me because of Heather, crazy as that sounds, and I guess he thinks whaling on me will help.

And if that's what it takes to end our one-sided feud, okay.

⚔ ⚔ ⚔

"Hey, Jakes. Hey, *sweetie*," Stanley yells, popping out from behind a far-off tree like some goofy, floppy-haired jack-in-the-box. He looks either nervous or excited, I can't tell which, and he keeps looking over his shoulder. "Come over here," he says.

I walk over to him as slowly as I can without going backward, because even though I want to get this fight over with, I am not exactly looking forward to it.

Who would be?

"Hey, Stanley," I say, nearing the tree. I am hoping that maybe Jared has decided to call the whole thing off, and Stanley is supposed to tell me.

And then—**SPROING!** Jared jumps down out of the tree like a big old stinkbug landing on an ant, if that's what stinkbugs do.

And we go rolling across the grass.

POW, POW! Jared punches me in the side, right where my poor skinny ribs are sticking out.

And I grab hold of his shirt and try to get in a punch or two of my own.

THUNK! THUNK!

My fist connects first with Jared's nose by accident, and then it sinks into his stomach, and Jared grunts. He is madder than ever now, and a little bit surprised that I am fighting back, judging by what I can see of the look on his face.

I would hit him again, only I never get the chance because we are rolling around on the ground some more, and all our arms are busy.

And all of a sudden, my mouth is full of Eustace B. Pennypacker's memorial grass—and some of his dirt, too, as Jared grinds my face into the lawn. "*Fuh*," I say, trying to spit it out.

"No spitting," Stanley cries, as if he is the referee, and this is supposed to be some really fair fight.

Yeah, right!

I would explain to them that I'm *not* spitting, only I never get the chance.

"I'll teach you not to spit on me," Jared says—

and he wrestles me onto my back and gets ready to spit in my face.

IN MY FACE!

As if spitting on a person will teach that person not to spit!

I would point out how messed-up this is, only I do not get the chance.

There is a roaring sound in my ears, and I shut my eyes and *especially my mouth*, and I get ready for the worst, only the worst never happens.

Instead, the roaring sound grows louder and louder, and I suddenly realize that it is kids, kids, and more kids, and they are swarming around us: Kevin McKinley, and Corey Robinson, who is supposed to be at swim practice, and Fiona McNulty, and Emma McGraw, and Heather Patton, who accidentally started the whole thing and doesn't even know it, and Annie Pat Masterson.

There are other kids here too, from different classes, and I don't even know their names.

How did they find out?

Stanley. I just know it. That's why he was looking over his shoulder!

Maybe he's not so bad after all.

"Get off him, Jared," Kevin shouts, grabbing Jared by the neck of his sweaty red T-shirt. "You're huge compared to EllRay. It's just not right," he yells.

But Jared wriggles away.

"Big meanie," Emma says, aiming a kick or two toward Jared's shins, which I wish she wouldn't do, because how does that make *me* look?

But Emma can't help herself. She is what my dad would call "a hothead." He says it like it's a bad thing.

"Oh, poor Jared," Heather cries out to the excited crowd of kids. "Look, his nose is bleeding!"

And those are the magic words, I guess, especially coming from *her*, because Jared suddenly lets me go.

I scramble to my feet before he changes his mind.

"You bully," Heather says, whirling to face me. "Why don't you pick on someone your own size, Ell-Ray Jakes?"

Which is when everyone starts to laugh.

Including Jared Matthews, luckily!

And *poof*, just like that our fight is over.

✳ 15 ✳

SURPRISE

"Everyone all set?" my dad asks us very early the next morning, after buckling Alfie into her car seat, because—we are on our way to Disneyland!

This will be the best treat ever.

And I earned it the hard way. I am so sore I can barely walk—but Disneyland will cure me.

"*I'm* all set," Alfie announces. She is dressed up in her favorite outfit: ruffled shirt, pink skirt, lacy white socks, and pink sneakers. "I'm going to meet Minnie Mouse," she tells us, looking excited, but also a little scared. "And she's famous."

"*Maybe* you'll meet Minnie," my mom tells her, I guess because she doesn't want Alfie to be disappointed if Minnie Mouse is on vacation in Cabo or something.

"I'll meet her, all wight," Alfie says grimly.

And for everyone's sake, I hope Minnie is on the job today.

"Well, let's keep our fingers crossed," Dad says, sounding a lot more excited than I thought he would. He's even wearing a shirt and sweater instead of a tie. "But leave some room, EllRay," he adds. "Because we're picking someone else up."

"Who?" Alfie asks.

"Yeah, who?" I ask.

My dad looks at me over his shoulder and smiles. "It's a surprise," he says, speaking mainly to me.

And it really, really is.

"Hey, Jared," I say a few minutes later, trying to make my voice sound normal as Jared Matthews clambers into the backseat of our car. This leaves me sitting in the middle, exactly where I hate to sit.

This is like a nightmare come true.

Jared and I accidentally solve everything all by ourselves, but it's for nothing? We have that stupid fight, but then they throw us together for a whole entire day?

I guess the grown-ups don't know it, but that's like expecting Jared and me to walk across a bridge that we just built out of white paste and Popsicle sticks.

We are **DOOMED!**

"Jared, we called your parents on Thursday night to suggest that you join us," Dad says as Jared buckles himself in. "And they agreed that it was a good way for you and EllRay to get to know each other a little better. Ms. Sanchez thought so, too. But we decided to keep it a secret—from both of you."

Okay. They called Jared's parents on Thursday night—*before* our big fight on Friday in Eustace B. Pennypacker Memorial Park.

Of course, the grown-ups haven't heard about the fight yet, I remind myself. For now, at least, it's still stealth. All they know is that he might have tripped me once. But the side of Jared's nose where I accidentally socked him yesterday afternoon is black and blue, I am secretly glad to see.

"Hey," he says to Alfie and me in greeting, not knowing where to look. He touches his sore nose. "I told my folks I fell off my skateboard," he whispers, before I can even ask.

In the front seat, Mom opens her purse, pulls out her little lipstick mirror, and peeks back at Jared and me—probably to see if we are silently strangling each other yet.

So far so good, Mom. Mostly because I'm still in shock.

"Who's that?" Aflie says, taking her wet thumb out of her mouth and waving it toward Jared with some suspicion.

"Oh, sorry. This is Jared Matthews," I tell her,

making the introduction. "He's in my class at school. This is my little sister Alfleta," I say to Jared, introducing Alfie politely—just in case Mom and Dad are listening, which I'm sure they are. "It means '*beautiful elf*,'" I explain.

"Hi," Jared mumbles to Alfie.

Alfie scowls. "EllWay told me about you one time," she says to Jared. "He said you were the meanest boy in his class."

"*Alfleta*," Mom scolds from the front seat. "That's enough. Behave yourself."

"That's okay, Mrs. Jakes," Jared says. What a kiss-up!

"She didn't mean it, Mom," I fib.

"I did too mean it," Alfie objects loudly. "EllWay and me decided that boy is just as bad as Suzette." I can tell that Jared does not like being compared to a girl, but there's not much he can do about it.

"I thought you and Suzette were friends again," I say to Alfie.

"Oh yeah," she says, remembering. "But maybe not next week."

"Well, that's kind of like Jared and me," I say, hoping to shut her up. "We're okay now."

Temporarily, at least.

"All wight," she says, accepting this.

Jared and I look at each other for a second, but we don't say anything until my dad is on the freeway heading north, and Alfie has gone back to sucking her thumb and twiddling the end of a soft black braid. She stares dreamily out the car window at the hills racing by. She is nearly asleep.

"I know you didn't want me to come," Jared growls, keeping his voice low.

I think hard for a couple of minutes about what to tell him, because if I lie and say that I'm really happy he's here, maybe he will leave me alone for the rest of the year. Or for a few weeks, anyway,

Or I can tell him the truth and take my chances.

"Not really," I finally admit.

"Well, I didn't even *want* to come, when they told me this morning," Jared whispers gruffly. "So don't think you're doing me any favors. I don't owe you, EllRay."

"Everything all right back there?" Dad asks, glancing at us in his rearview mirror.

"Everything's fine," I report. "Alfie's asleep, and we're just talking quietly."

After Dad gets busy driving again, Jared and I exchange glares. "I'm glad Stanley told," he mutters, his voice even quieter than before. "That's why all those kids came running to the park yesterday. They wanted to see you get it, EllRay."

"They did not," I tell him, also keeping my voice low. "They didn't care *what* they saw, as long as it was something exciting, for a change. And anyway, maybe Stanley told because he likes to do stuff behind your back. And all those kids saw was *you*, getting a bloody nose. Even Heather Patton saw it," I remind him. "*You're welcome*," I add, trying for a little sarcasm.

My heart is thunking so hard in my chest that I can practically see it through my San Diego Padres T-shirt, the one Jared wishes he had, but at least I am defending myself again.

I think the days of me washing my hands for no reason are over.

Jared scowls, but he doesn't say anything more.

This is going to be some weird treat, that's for sure. My stomach is doing flip-flops already—and not the good, scary-ride kind.

Great plan, grown-ups! Just when most of the bad feelings between Jared and me were over *because* of our fight, which we both won, in a way, you went and made things worse by trying to make us have fun together.

Thanks a *lot*.

✳ **16** ✳

TEMPORARY

If there is one thing that no one likes about Disneyland, I remember about twenty minutes after we first walk down Main Street, it is the lines you have to wait in to get on the rides.

Long, boring, zigzagging lines.

Then, when you finally, finally get to the front of the line, all of a sudden there is a crazy scramble to jump on the ride, and then **WHOOSH**, the ride is over.

The *whoosh* part can be really fun, though—even when Jared Matthews is sitting there next to you like a tree stump, which sometimes happens because of the crazy scramble part.

Of course, Mom and Dad were probably planning on Jared going with me on every single ride. They probably imagined that we would slowly learn to like each other, and maybe even become friends, but even parents can't argue when the official ride people shoo you onto a ride when it's finally your turn. Not when there are a thousand people in line behind you.

As the morning goes on, though, even I have to admit that the invisible coating of ice that has been covering both Jared and me—like the candy coating on an M&M—is beginning to melt a little.

But then, just after lunch, "I want Minnie ears,"

Alfie starts whining after we have been in line for twenty minutes for the pirates ride, and Jared and I exchange worried looks.

"She has a meltdown every afternoon," I tell Jared gloomily. "She still takes naps, that's the thing."

"Who are you talking about?" Alfie asks, sounding suspicious.

"You stay in line," Dad tells Jared, Mom, and me. "I'll take Alfie and go find a Minnie hat."

"No, Warren," Mom says. "We'll all go with you. We have to stick together, or someone's going to get lost."

But it's *Disneyland*, I want to tell them as we get ready to lose our very good place in line. How bad could it be if a very-mature-for-his-age kid, like me, got lost? I could live here forever!

"I have an idea, Louise," Dad says. "I think Ell-Ray and Jared can be on their own for a while, if they promise to stick together. We could try it for an hour, maybe, and see how it goes."

We get to be alone? *In Disneyland?* I can hardly believe what I am hearing!

Even Jared is looking excited.

"I don't know," Mom says, looking worried.

"You could lend EllRay your cell phone," Dad suggests gently. "He'll call me on my cell every fifteen minutes to check in."

I'd call every minute if he asked me to!

Jared and I both hold our breath.

"Well, okay," Mom finally agrees as Alfie starts to tug her away from the line. "Here's my phone, EllRay. *Don't lose it.*"

Mom's cell phone is yellow, sparkly, and very girly, which is embarrassing, but I slip it into my deepest pocket and swap excited, happy glances with Jared, my temporary friend.

"We'll meet here in exactly one hour," Dad says, tapping his watch.

"Okay," I tell him.

"Okay," Jared mumbles happily.

And we're off!

✕　✕　✕

Being at Disneyland with Jared wasn't so bad, I think sleepily on the way home. In fact, I don't want to exaggerate or anything, but it was really, really fun.

There were no wedgies, no playing keep-away, no knuckle-grinding, no nothing.

And even though something bad will probably happen again next week, especially when the grown-ups hear about the fight at Eustace B. Penny-packer Memorial Park, a fight that to Jared and me is old news, things are okay for now.

And that's good enough for me!

WHAT HAPPENS TO ELLRAY IN HIS NEXT
ADVENTURE? TURN THE PAGE TO
READ A CHAPTER FROM

✳ ✳ ✳

MY CRYSTAL-CLEAR IDEA

On Monday night before bed, as my mom is giving Alfie her usual three-towel bath, I wander into Dad's home office to look around—because I kind of miss him.

Also, I usually don't get to go in there unless I'm in trouble.

Even though almost anyone would think that being a geology professor is boring, my dad's office is pretty cool. The wall opposite his desk is completely covered with wood shelves that are so narrow an apple would feel fat sitting there. All my dad's favorite small rock specimens are on these shelves, and each one is carefully labeled. The rocks are from all over the world—Asia, South America, North America—and he collected each specimen himself.

My dad has been *everywhere.*

My favorite shelves are the ones nearest the window, because those hold the crystals. Dad put the crystals there so that sunlight will shine on them first thing in the morning. He says it's a nice way to start the day.

Crystals grow on or in rocks, and they are like diamonds, only better—because they're much bigger, and they come in so many different colors: blue, green, red, orange, and yellow. Even the gray and brown crystals are awesome, not to mention the clear ones that are like ice that never melts.

And crystals look like somebody carved them, only they grew that way! Nature was the carver.

But my dad was the guy who collected them, and he has a story for each one.

My dad's rock specimens are like his life scrapbook, practically.

I just wish some of the kids in my class could see them. Maybe then they'd stop bragging about their dads' ATVs, and their money, and their solid gold jewelry, and how everything's a contest that they are winning.

The kids in my class would see how awesome my dad's crystals are.

And I would win.

That's when I get my crystal-clear idea.

I will borrow six of my dad's crystals—only six!—from his office this very minute, then sneak them up to my room. Then I'll put each crystal in its very own white tube sock for protection, so they won't get knocked around inside my backpack when I take them to school tomorrow.

But before that, I'll spread out the other crystals on my dad's shelf so Mom won't see any empty places in case she goes into the office before he gets home late tomorrow night.

Then tomorrow, Tuesday, I will ask Ms. Sanchez if I can show everyone the crystals, and talk—okay, brag—about them, and she will say yes, because crystals are so scientific and beautiful. Everyone in my class will be totally amazed and impressed, and it will be the best Tuesday I ever had in my life. I might even get extra credit!

Then I will take all the crystals home tomorrow afternoon and sneak them back onto the shelf so they will be there when he gets home. He will never know that six of his crystals took a little field trip to Oak Glen Elementary School—to make both him and me look good.

There is *no way* this plan can go wrong!